First U.S. edition 2016

Library of Congress Catalog Card Number 2015941708
ISBN 978-0-7636-7837-1

16 17 18 19 20 21 CCP 10 9 8 7 6 5 4 3 2 1

Printed in Shenzhen, Guangdong, China

This book was typeset in Futura.
The illustrations were done in mixed media.

Candlewick Press
99 Dover Street
Somerville, Massachusetts 02144

visit us at www.candlewick.com

CANDLEWICK PRESS

ANTHONY BROWNE

FRIDA AND BEAR
PLAY THE SHAPE GAME!

HANNE BARTHOLIN

Frida loved to draw.

And so did Bear.
But one day Bear couldn't think of anything to draw.
"What can I draw, Frida?" he said.

Frida drew a shape
and gave it to Bear.

"Try to turn this shape into something, Bear,"
said Frida.

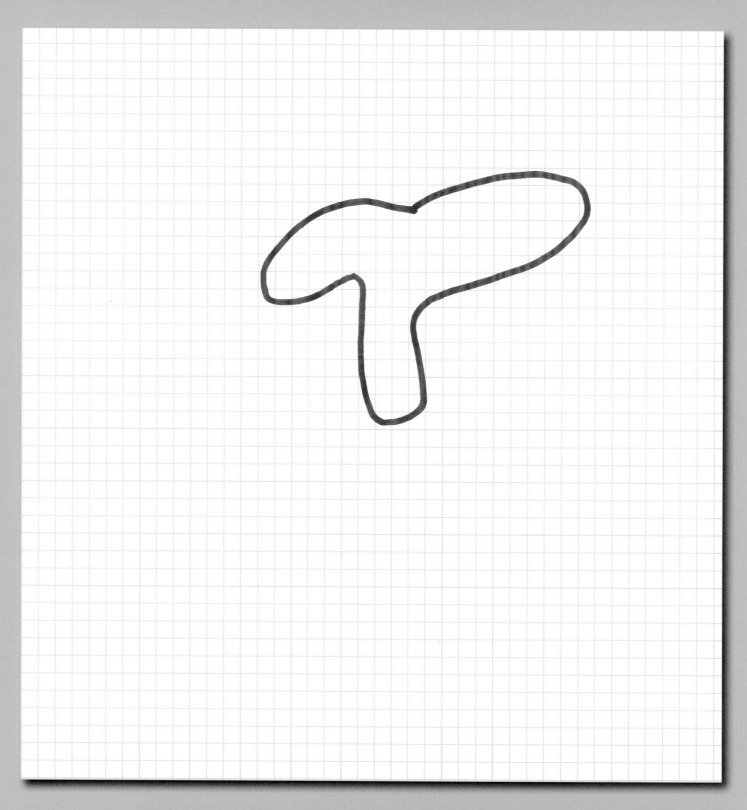

Bear looked at the shape . . . and started to draw.

He turned the shape into a puppy.

"It's my turn now, Frida," said Bear.

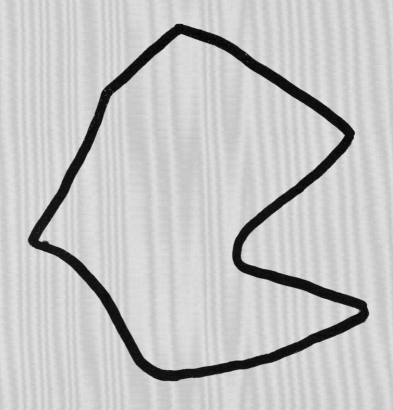

So he drew a shape and passed it to Frida.

Frida turned it into a fish.

"Oooh, that's a big fish!" said Bear.

It was Frida's turn again,
so she drew another shape for Bear.

Bear thought for a while, then turned it into a pig.
"That's funny!" said Frida, laughing.

Bear made another shape.

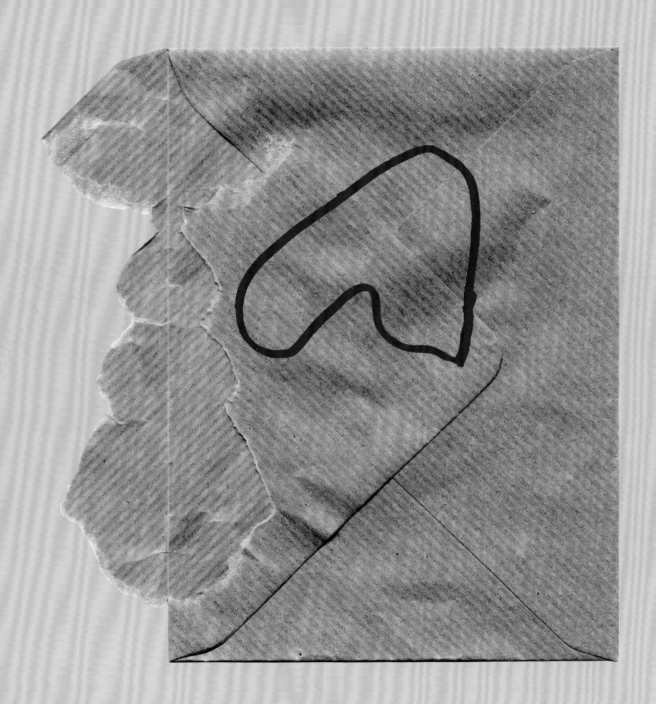

Frida turned it into a funny little man.

Frida gave Bear a piece of wrapping paper.

"I know what that looks like," said Bear,
and he began to draw.

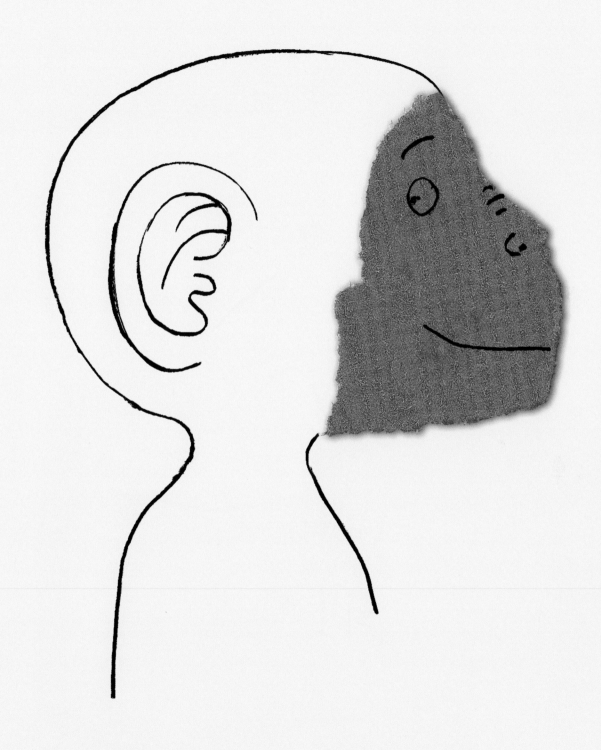

"A monkey!" said Frida. "He looks cheeky."

Bear took a twig out of his pocket
and gave it to Frida.
"I wonder what that could be?" said Frida.
"Ah, I know!"

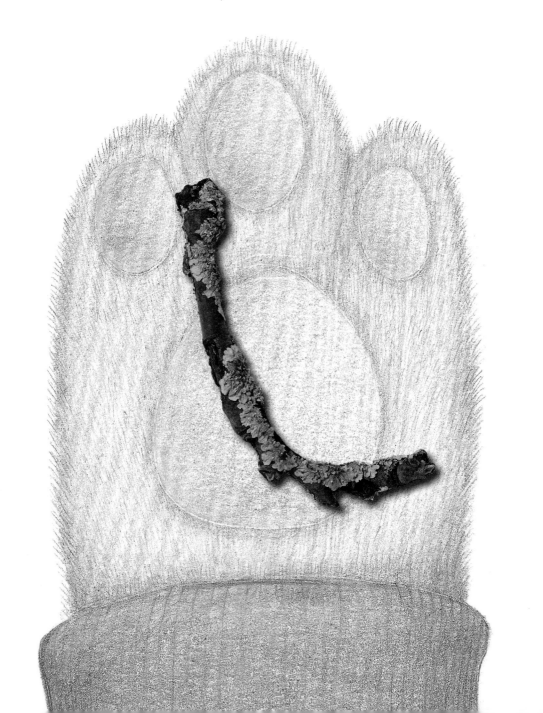

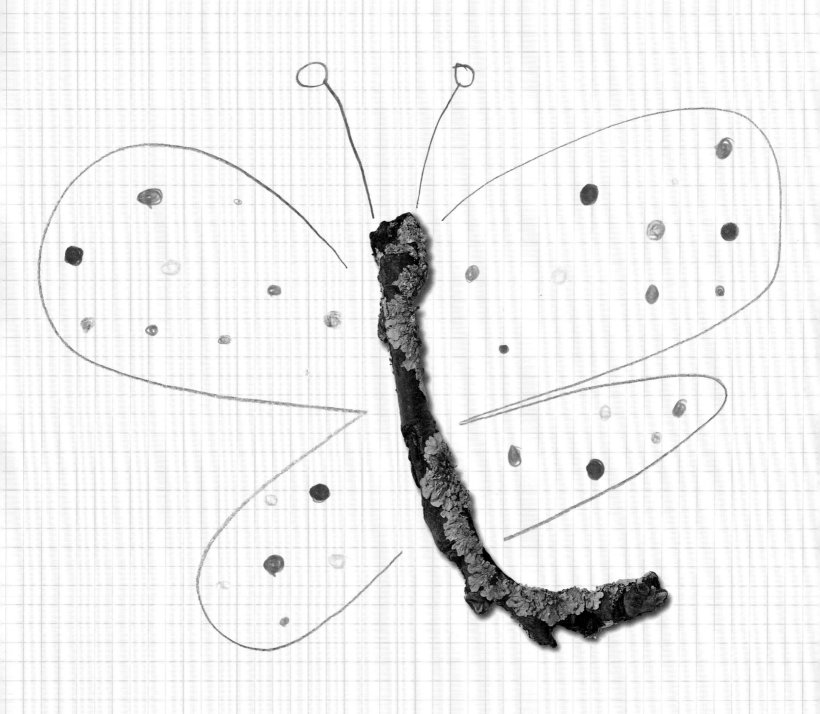

And Frida turned it into a butterfly.
"That's lovely!" said Bear. "Well done."

Frida and Bear love this game

and play it every day.

Look at all the pictures Frida and Bear
have drawn!

Why don't you draw some shapes and play?